KU-252-000

MARC BROWN

ARTHUR BABY-SITS

RED FOX

With love and thanks to some great readers and writers:
Barbara Bush; Ms. Cassell's class in Terre Haute, Indiana;
and Mary Etta Bitter's class in Lakewood, Ohio

A Red Fox Book

Published by Random House Children's Books
20 Vauxhall Bridge Road, London SW1V 2SA

A division of Random House UK Ltd
London Melbourne Sydney Auckland
Johannesburg and agencies throughout the world

Copyright © 1992 Marc Brown

1 3 5 7 9 10 8 6 4 2

First published in the United States of America by
Little, Brown & Company and simultaneously in Canada by
Little, Brown & Company (Canada) Ltd 1992

First published in Great Britain by Red Fox 1997

This book is sold subject to the condition that it shall not, by way
of trade or otherwise, be lent, resold, hired out, or otherwise
circulated without the publisher's prior consent in any form of
binding or cover other than that in which it is published and
without a similar condition including this condition being
imposed on the subsequent purchaser.

The right of Marc Brown to be identified as the author and
illustrator of this work has been asserted by him in accordance
with the Copyright, Designs and Patents Act, 1988.

Printed in Hong Kong

RANDOM HOUSE UK Limited Reg. No. 954009

ISBN 0 09 921902 6

Arthur's sister D.W. had a problem.
"The Tibble twins are visiting again, and they're driving
me crazy!" she said. "They're everywhere I go."
"Oh, they can't be that bad," said Arthur.
"How would you know?" said D.W.

Later that afternoon, Arthur and D.W. took Kate for a walk.

"Look!" shouted the Tibble twins. "There's D.W.!"

"Oh, no!" said D.W. "Quick, let's hide."

Mrs Tibble looked worried.

"I'm in a terrible pickle," she said. "I need a baby-sitter for my grandsons tonight, and I can't find one anywhere."

"Arthur will do it!" said D.W. "He baby-sits me all the time."

"Oh, Arthur, you're a life-saver!" said Mrs Tibble. "I'll call your mother and arrange it right now."

"Baby-sitting is such a big responsibility," said Arthur.
"I'm a little bit nervous."
"You'll do a good job," said Mother.
"We'll be right here if you want to call us," said Father.
"Here's my crash helmet," said D.W. "You'll need it!"
"Why?" asked Arthur. "Are you coming along?"
"You think *I'm* trouble?" said D.W. "Just wait."

On the way, Arthur walked past the Sugar Bowl.

"Hey, Arthur," called Buster, "where are you going?"

"I'm on my way to baby-sit for Mrs Tibble," said Arthur.

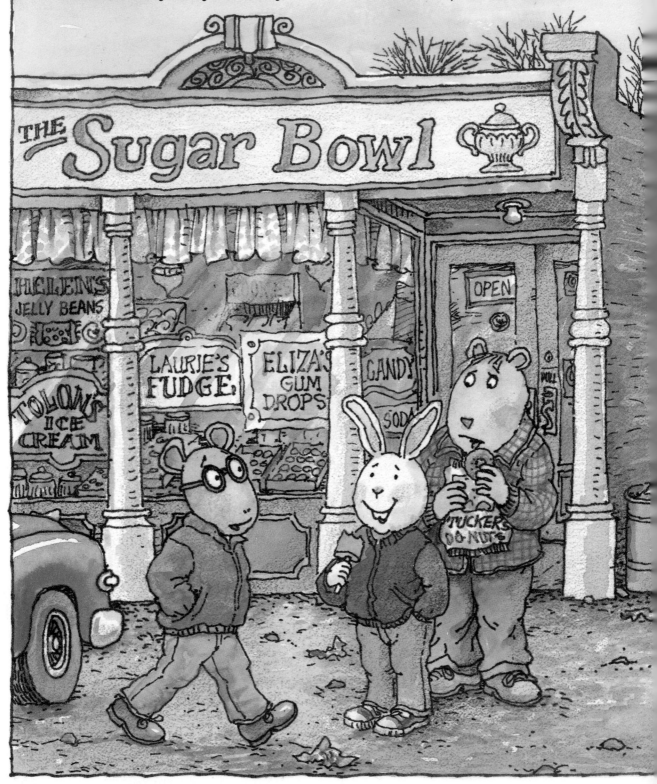

"Not the terrible Tibble twins!" gasped Prunella. "My sister baby-sat for them once. And *once* was enough."

"You can always back out," said Buster, ". . . while you're still alive."

"Don't worry," said Francine. "It will be just like baby-sitting D.W. and Baby Kate."

Arthur remembered what that was like!

Now he was really worried.

Mrs Tibble was waiting for Arthur.

"I'm so glad you're here," she said. "And so are the twins.
This is little Tommy in red, and Timmy's in blue. Almost
bedtime, darlings! I'll be back soon."

"Very soon, I hope," said Arthur.

"Nighty-night, Grammy," said the twins sweetly.

The phone rang. It was D.W.

"I'm calling with some advice," she said. "Calm them down
with a quiet game . . . like cards."

"Thanks," said Arthur. "Bye."

"How about a nice quiet game of cards?" asked Arthur.

"Great!" said the twins.

"We know a really good card game . . ." said Tommy.

"Fifty-two card pick-up!" they screamed.
Just then the phone rang again. It was D.W.
"It sounds like they're out of control," she said. "You need
to show them who's boss!"
"Thanks a lot," said Arthur.

"Let's play cowboys!" said Tommy.

"I'll be the sheriff," said Arthur, "because I'm the boss."

"And we'll be the bad guys," said Timmy.

The next time the phone rang, Timmy answered it.
"Arthur can't come to the phone right now," he said.
"He's all tied up."
"Time for hide-and-seek!" called Tommy. "You'll never
find us!"

When Arthur finally got loose, he searched and searched.
"If I don't find them soon," he thought, "I'll be in big trouble."

Just then the phone rang again.

"What's going on over there?" asked D.W. "Shouldn't they be in bed?"

"I can't talk now," said Arthur. "I'm looking for the twins."

"You mean you've lost them?" shouted D.W.

"Not exactly," he said. "I just can't find them."

"You're in really big trouble!" said D.W. "What are you going to do?"

Just then Arthur noticed the curtains wiggling.
"You'll see," he said. "I just hope I find them before the
swamp thing does!" he added loudly.
"Swamp thing?" asked Tommy from behind the curtain.

"Yes, the one that comes out on nights just like tonight," Arthur said. "Sit down and I'll tell you all about it." Arthur used his spookiest voice. "Once upon a time in a dark spooky swamp, there lived a horrible, big, slimy, stinky green swamp thing," he began.

"You mean like a monster?" Tommy asked meekly.

"Exactly," said Arthur, "with long, sharp teeth. And the swamp thing realized it was very, very hungry," said Arthur. "It left the swamp in search of dinner."

"What did it like to eat?" Timmy asked in a shaky voice.

"Boys," said Arthur. "Especially twin boys."

The twins moved closer to Arthur.
"The swamp thing began to moan from hunger," continued
Arthur, "until it came to a big old house, just like this one."
"I can hear footsteps!" cried Timmy.

"It's only your imagination," said Arthur. "Do you want to sit on my lap?"
"Well, just for a minute," said Timmy.

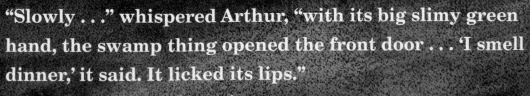

"Slowly . . ." whispered Arthur, "with its big slimy green hand, the swamp thing opened the front door . . . 'I smell dinner,' it said. It licked its lips."

"Help!" screamed the twins.

"It's coming in *our* front door!" yelled Timmy.

Just then the door *did* open, and the lights came on.

"I'm home!" said Mrs Tibble. "And look at my little angels.
Arthur must be a wonderful baby-sitter."

"He's not scared of anything," said Timmy.

"And he tells great stories, too!" said Tommy. "We want him
to baby-sit us again."

The twins hugged Arthur good night.

Then Mrs Tibble paid Arthur and thanked him for doing
such a good job.

When Arthur got home, D.W. was still up.
"You're home early," she said. "Have you been fired?"
"No," said Arthur. "Baby-sitting isn't so bad. Mrs Tibble thinks I'm pretty good at it. Now she wants me to baby-sit the twins every afternoon right here at our house. And . . .

"... since you know so much about baby-sitting, *you* can help!"